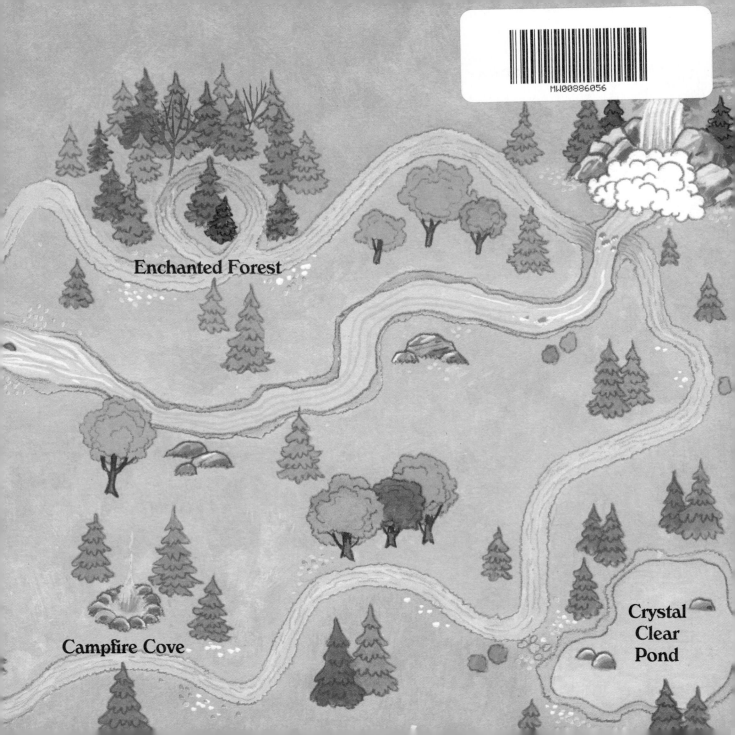

Enchanted Forest

Campfire Cove

Crystal
Clear
Pond

Published in Nashville, Tennessee, by Thomas Nelson, Inc.,
Publishers, and distributed in Canada by Word Communications,
Ltd., Richmond, British Columbia.

ISBN 0-7852-8344-7

Printed in the United States of America

1 2 3 4 5 6 — 99 98 97 96 95 94

The Band of Merry Bandits

Carrie & Renee Minirth
with their dad, Buffalo Frank

as told to Christine Harder Tangvald

Illustrated by
Jim Conway

A JANET THOMA BOOK

THOMAS NELSON PUBLISHERS
Nashville • Atlanta • London • Vancouver

All the campers at Big Creek Ranch hurried to sit around the crackling fire at Campfire Cove. Each night they sang songs and waited for their special friend Buffalo Frank to tell a tale of long ago.

"Buffalo Frank," said one girl, "we brought you this beautiful bouquet of daisies. We picked them for you over by Indian Skeleton Rock!"

"Why, thank you," said Buffalo Frank in his deep rumbly tumbly

voice. "They are mighty pretty!" His blue eyes twinkled and he smiled a big smile through his thick white beard.

"Buffalo Frank, is there a story about Indian Skeleton Rock?" asked the children.

"You bet!" said Buffalo Frank. "And a scary story it is!" He laid the bouquet of daisies on a sassafras stump. Then he sat down and leaned toward the fire. He began to tell this story:

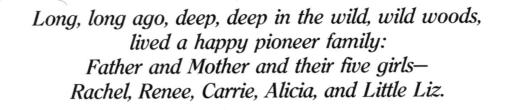

*Long, long ago, deep, deep in the wild, wild woods,
lived a happy pioneer family:
Father and Mother and their five girls—
Rachel, Renee, Carrie, Alicia, and Little Liz.*

One cloudy day Carrie and Renee were walking along Pole Cat Road, down by Indian Skeleton Rock.

"What are we going to do?" asked Renee.

"Mother's birthday party is tonight, and we don't have a present for her yet."

Carrie kicked a pebble with her shoe, sending it tumbling and bouncing ahead of her. "I don't know," she said, "but we better think of something . . . and fast!"

"I want Mother's present to be special," said Renee, "more special than anything else in the whole wide world."

"Me too," said Carrie as she kicked the pebble again. "But what can it be?"

Bounce, bounce, bounce went the pebble.

Bounce, bounce, clunk!

The pebble hit the side of Indian Skeleton Rock.

As Carrie bent over to pick it up, a big white daisy tickled her nose.

That gave Carrie an idea. "I know," she said, holding up the daisy.

"Let's pick Mother a beautiful bouquet of flowers! She loves flowers!"

"That's a great idea! She loves flowers—especially white daisies and black-eyed Susans," said Renee.

"Then it's settled," said Carrie. "I will pick Mother the biggest, most beautiful bouquet of white daisies in the whole wide world."

"And I will pick her the biggest, most beautiful bouquet of black-eyed Susans in the whole wide world," said Renee.

Off they went.

They picked their way around Indian Skeleton Rock and started across the Green, Green Meadow.

"Only pick the most beautiful flowers," said Carrie.

"And the ones with the longest stems," said Renee.

They picked and walked right over the bank and down to the edge of Short Creek. Then they tiptoed across the steep stepping stones right through the rushing, gushing waters.

"Be careful, Carrie!" said Renee as Carrie dropped a white daisy into the water. The girls watched as the flower whirled and twirled and swirled, clear down over Splish Splash Falls.

They jumped to the shore on the other side,
and started up the winding path. On and on the girls
wandered—so intent on picking the biggest, most beautiful
bouquets of flowers in the whole wide world that they forgot to pay
attention to where they were going.

The sky turned pink. Then red. Then violet. Dark shadows of
evening began to creep longer and longer over the valley.

12

But the girls did not notice.

They picked and walked deep into the shadow of Rough Rocky Ridge.

"I'm getting tired," said Renee. "And I simply cannot carry any more flowers."

"Neither can I," said Carrie. "Besides, it is starting to get dark. We better get home or we will be late for Mother's party."

Carrie and Renee turned to go home.
The girls looked up the ridge.
The girls looked down the ridge.
They looked all around Rough Rocky Ridge.
But all they saw were deep dark shadows.
"Where are we?" cried Carrie.
"I don't know!" said Renee. "I . . . I . . . think we might be lost!"
"I know we are lost!" cried Carrie.
Just then the girls heard something in the shadows.
Rustle, rustle, rustle. "What's that noise?" whispered Renee.

Rustle, rustle, rustle.

"I don't know," said Carrie, "but I don't like it."

Then Carrie saw him. He had two pointy ears . . . and two beady eyes . . . and he was wearing a big black mask!

"Run! Run!" shouted Carrie. "It's a bandit!"

Both girls dropped their flowers and spun around to escape down the hill, but . . .

There was another bandit! And another! And another!

They all had pointy ears . . . and beady eyes . . . and big black masks!

16

"We're surrounded. We're surrounded by bandits!" cried Renee. "Let's make a run for it."

"Wait a minute," shouted Carrie. "That bandit looks like . . . a raccoon." She rushed over to the biggest bandit of the bunch. "You look more like a rascal than a bandit, now that I see you up close."

The furry raccoon seemed to smile at Carrie. "Let's call him Rascal," Carrie said.

The big raccoon began to twist and turn around as if he were

18

dancing. Carrie laughed. Renee laughed. The raccoons seemed to laugh too. Carrie and Renee scoped up their flowers.

Soon the girls and the raccoons were twirling and rolling down the grassy slope together. At the bottom of the hill Carrie stopped playing. "We are still lost, Renee," she said. "What shall we do?"

19

Rascal took hold of Carrie's sleeve and tugged.
Carrie frowned. "What is it, Rascal? What's the matter?"
Rascal tugged on her sleeve again. Then he shuffled off down the hill.

"Oh, Renee!" said Carrie. "I think he wants us to follow him. Maybe he knows the way home!"

Rascal nodded his head. All his friends joined him, ready to lead the girls home.

They hurried out of the shadow of Rough Rocky Ridge—and scurried past the deep, dark forest.

They went down the winding path to the edge of Short Creek.

Rascal Raccoon and the other merry bandits hopped across the steep stepping stones.

The two girls tiptoed across the rushing, gushing waters of Short Creek.

"Be careful, Carrie!" said Renee as Carrie dropped another white daisy into the water, and they watched it whirl and twirl and swirl clear down over Splish Splash Falls.

Up the bank they went on the other side.
Across Green, Green Meadow Rascal and his friends hurried.

"Here it is!" cried Carrie. "Here is Indian Skeleton Rock. Now we know exactly where we are!"

"Oh, thank you, Rascal," said Carrie. She gave him a big, big hug.

24

"Oh, thank you, Rascal," said Renee. She gave him an even bigger hug.

Rascal blinked his eyes. Then he turned and took his band of merry bandits across Green, Green Meadow and disappeared into the evening shadows.

Carrie and Renee arrived home just in time for Mother's birthday party.

"We were so worried about you," said Father. "Where have you been?"

"We picked these flowers for you, Mother," the girls said together.

"Oh, my!" said Mother. "I think these are the most beautiful flowers in the whole wide world! I hope it wasn't too much trouble to pick them."

Carrie looked at Renee.
Renee looked at Carrie.
They began to laugh out loud.
"Oh, no, Mother. It was no trouble at all."

"Wow! That was a great story, Buffalo Frank!" said all the children around the campfire.

"Is it true? Was there really a raccoon named Rascal with a band of merry bandits?"

"That's what some folks say," said Buffalo Frank.
Then Buffalo Frank leaned in toward the fire and his face became very, very serious.

"You know, some folks say that

    —on a cold dark night
    —when the big round moon shines so bright,
    —if you listen with all your might

you can still hear Rascal and his band of merry bandits hurrying and scurrying here and there and everywhere!"

"Really?" whispered the children.

"Well, that's what some folks say!"

Long, long ago, deep, deep in the wild, wild woods, lived a
HAPPY PIONEER FAMILY

Father   Mother   Rachel   Renee   Carrie   Alicia   Little Liz